To our new little peanut, Luna.
May you always find your courage
(and eat your veggies).

Books may be purchased in quantity and/or special sales by contacting the publisher, Louie's Little Lessons, at hello@louieslittlelessons.com.

Published in San Diego, California by Louie's Little Lessons. Louie's Little Lessons is a registered trademark.

Illustrations by: Greg Bishop
Interior Design by: Ron Eddy
Cover Design by: Greg Bishop and Ron Eddy
Editing by: Julie Breihan

Printed in the China

ISBN-13: 978-0-9981936-1-8

Louie's Little Lessons

I CAN'T EAT THIS STUFF

written by **Liz Fletcher**   illustrated by **Greg Bishop**

Louie flies as fast as lightning,
Up, up, and away!

Did you know that
   he's a superhero?
He loves to save the day!

He must stay strong and healthy.
Have you ever seen him flex?

Whoa! Take
a look!

Let's see your
muscles next!

Louie uses his superpowers
To finish up his chores.

Then it's time to go outside
And wrestle dinosaurs!

Uh-oh (*grumble, grumble*).
It must be time for dinner.

Louie's energy is gettin' low,
And he's looking a little thinner.

How about a
    chocolate sundae
Topped with gooey
    marshmallow fluff?"

"Hi, Louie. I'm Bell,
   And we vegetables must admit
   That sugary foods can be bad for you
   If you want to stay powerful and fit."

"Bell's right. Hey, I'm Broc.
I look like a tiny green tree.
I keep your heart and
muscles strong.

You definitely want
to eat me."

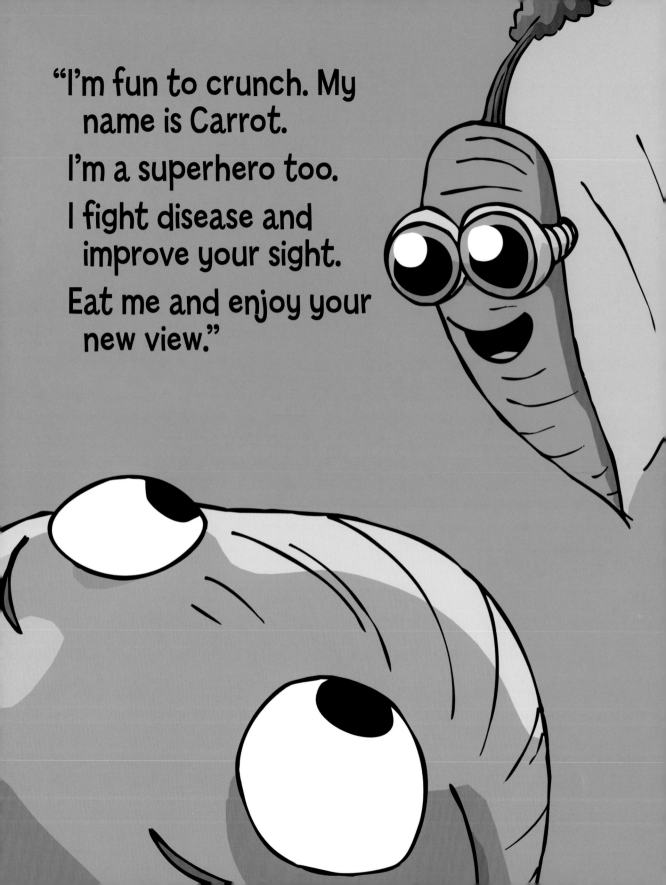

"I'm fun to crunch. My name is Carrot.

I'm a superhero too.

I fight disease and improve your sight.

Eat me and enjoy your new view."

"Well, Broc and Carrot are cool,
But I, too, am a real winner.
I'm very tasty, and I keep you healthy.
Try sweet potatoes for dinner!"

"I may be little, but I sure am fierce.
Hopefully you'll agree.
I keep your blood and bones in shape.
My name is Mr. Pea."

Hmmm, Louie thinks.

I just don't know what to do.

I want to stay strong
and healthy,

But I'm unsure about
trying something new.

Louie fastens his cape tightly.
He can feel his courage and might.

"Okay!" he says.
"I'll try them.

"Wait a second . . . I like them!
They actually taste really great,

And I'm starting to feel extra super.
Yum! I think I'll
   clean my plate!"

Now Louie can't wait to eat his vegetables
Because they're a superhero fuel!

"They give me
energy and
keep me strong.

Change is so very important.
Louie is glad he tried something new.
He loves eating his vegetables,
And you know what? You will too!

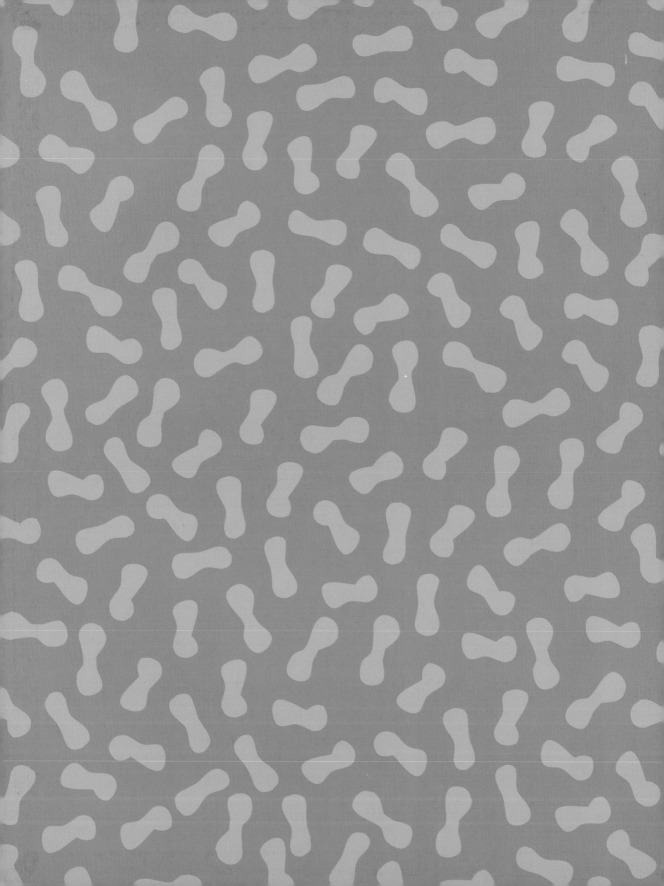